Little Patriot Press

# HOUSE MOUSE
# SENATE MOUSE

PROUDLY PRESENTING

THE SQUEAKER OF THE HOUSE

and

THE SENATE MOUSE-JORITY LEADER

THE CAPITOL

HOW OUR LAWS ARE MADE

By Peter W. Barnes and Cheryl Shaw Barnes

Little Patriot Press® is a registered trademark of Salem Communications Holding Corporation
Regnery® is a registered trademark of Salem Communications Holding Corporation

Cataloging-in-Publication data on file with the Library of Congress

ISBN 978-1-59698-790-6

Published in the United States by
Little Patriot Press
An imprint of Regnery Publishing
A Division of Salem Media Group
300 New Jersey Ave NW
Washington, DC 20001
www.Regnery.com

Manufactured in the United States of America

10 9 8 7 6 5 4

Books are available in quantity for promotional or premium use. For information on discounts and terms, please visit our website: www.Regnery.com.

Distributed to the trade by
Perseus Distribution
www.perseusdistribution.com

This book is dedicated to Murphy,
my beloved 23-year-old cat,
who sat many hours on the drawings on these pages
—he was loving company.

–C. S. B.

★ ★ ★

Find George Washingtail hidden in each illustration.

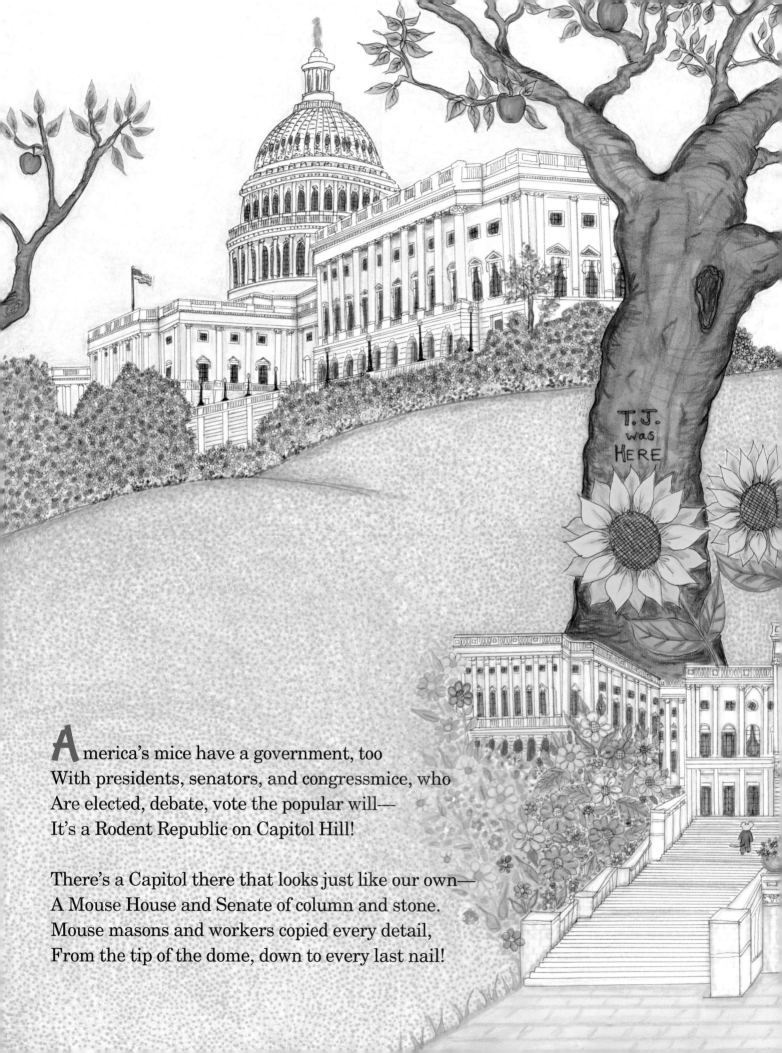

**A**merica's mice have a government, too
With presidents, senators, and congressmice, who
Are elected, debate, vote the popular will—
It's a Rodent Republic on Capitol Hill!

There's a Capitol there that looks just like our own—
A Mouse House and Senate of column and stone.
Mouse masons and workers copied every detail,
From the tip of the dome, down to every last nail!

One day in Moussouri, a wonderful state,
A teacher, Miss Tuftmouse, at about half past eight,
Told her class, "Settle down, everyone, and sit up straight!
There's a special assignment, and it must not be late!

"The class, all together, for worse or for better,
Must write to our Congress an interesting letter.
You ought to get started, not later, but soon,
For you must turn it in by this Thursday at noon!"

Well the children, excited, did not waste a minute,
Working hard on their letter and what to put in it.
For three classes straight, they wrote and they read.
Then the letter was finished, and here's what it said:

Miss Tuftmouse, of course, gave the letter an "A"
And mailed it to Congress the very next day.
It went to the mail room, where the mail comes in crates,
From Moussouri, Moussissippi, and other mouse states.

The Postmouster took it to Longworth McMouse,
The capable, confident Squeaker of the House.
A copy was rushed across to the Senate,
To the Mouse-jority Leader, Russell Mouse Bennett.

Then Longworth called Russell as quick as a blink:
"A National Cheese—well, what do you think?"
"Good idea!" the Mouse-jority Leader said back.
"We'll draw up a bill to get it on track!"

To make a new law, Congress starts with a "bill,"
A document written with care and with skill.
To find the right words, mouse assistants begin
With the Library of Congress, and the books found within.

Ways and Means Committee Room

Next a "committee" considers the bill,
For it just isn't finished or ready until
The members discuss it, make changes and more,
Then finally send it along to the floor.

That's the floor of each chamber, the Senate and House—
It's where each senator and each congressmouse
Gets to vote on the bill, and if enough do,
The president signs it if he likes it too.

Senate Chamber

But it's not always easy for all to agree
On just what a bill should do, say, or be.
For example, the bill for a National Cheese
Caused a big disagreement, a lot of unease!

Some mice wanted Cheddar to take the top spot.
Some mice wanted Roquefort, but others said not.
Some said Parmesan, some couldn't care less—
So many opinions, and such a big mess!

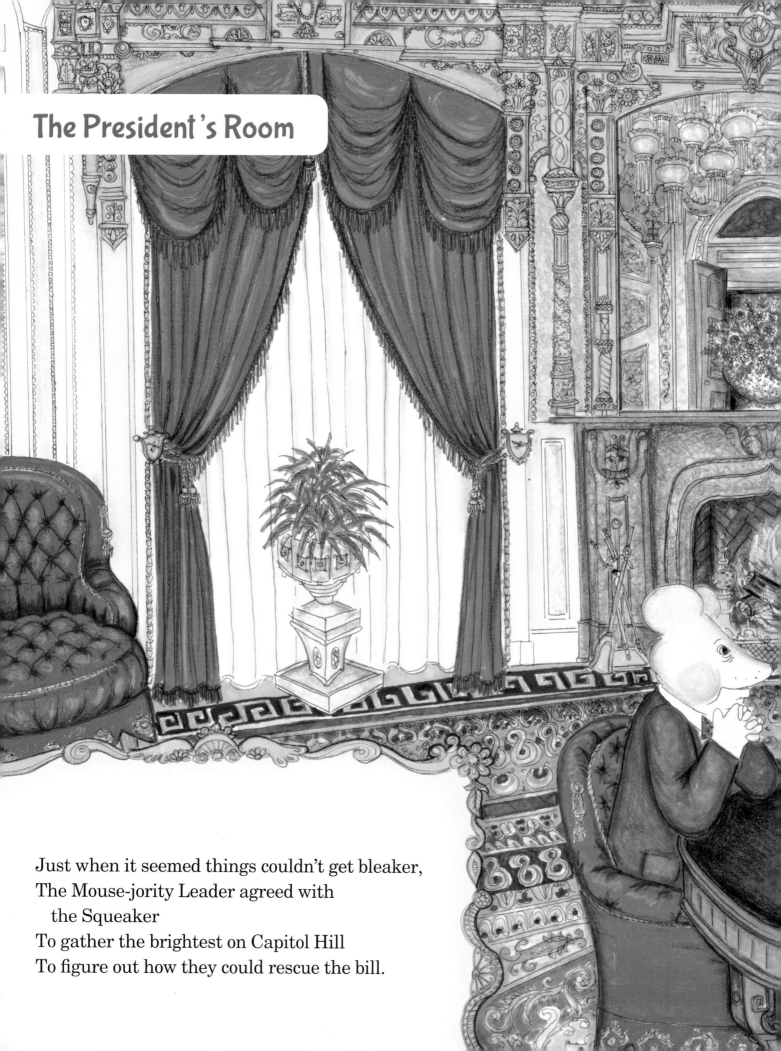

# The President's Room

Just when it seemed things couldn't get bleaker,
The Mouse-jority Leader agreed with
  the Squeaker
To gather the brightest on Capitol Hill
To figure out how they could rescue the bill.

The Rotunda was packed—a good place to meet—
When Senator Thurmouse rose to his feet.
The oldest and wisest in Congress by years—
The Squeaker, the Leader, the rest were all ears!

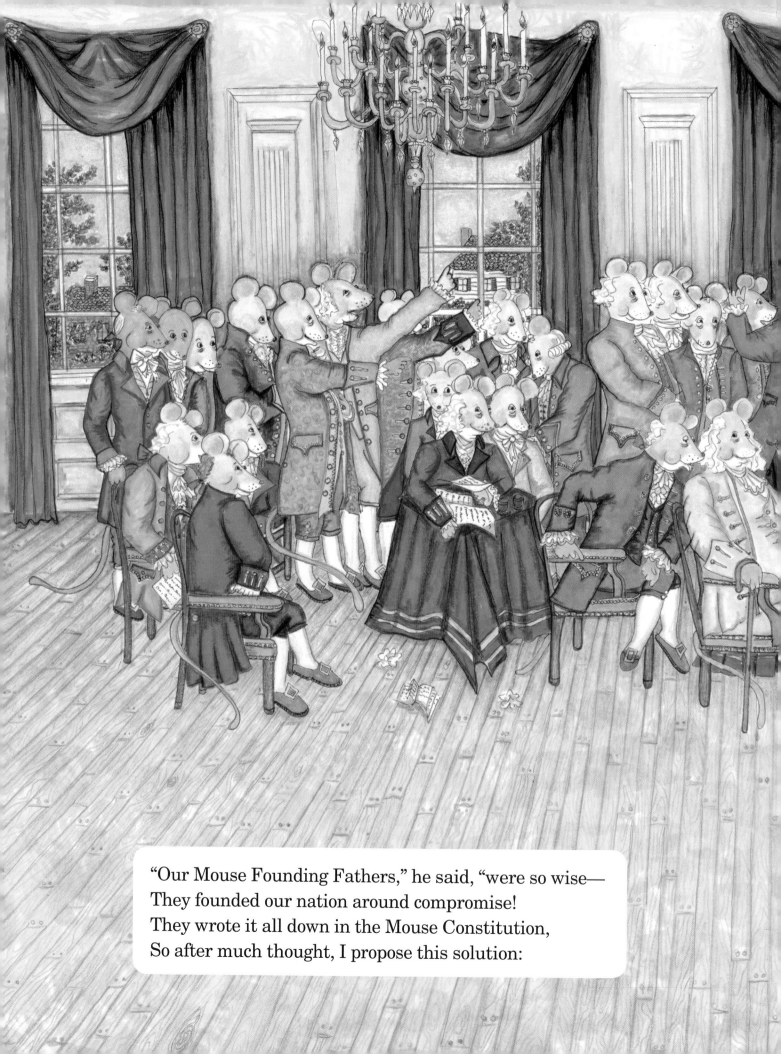

"Our Mouse Founding Fathers," he said, "were so wise—
They founded our nation around compromise!
They wrote it all down in the Mouse Constitution,
So after much thought, I propose this solution:

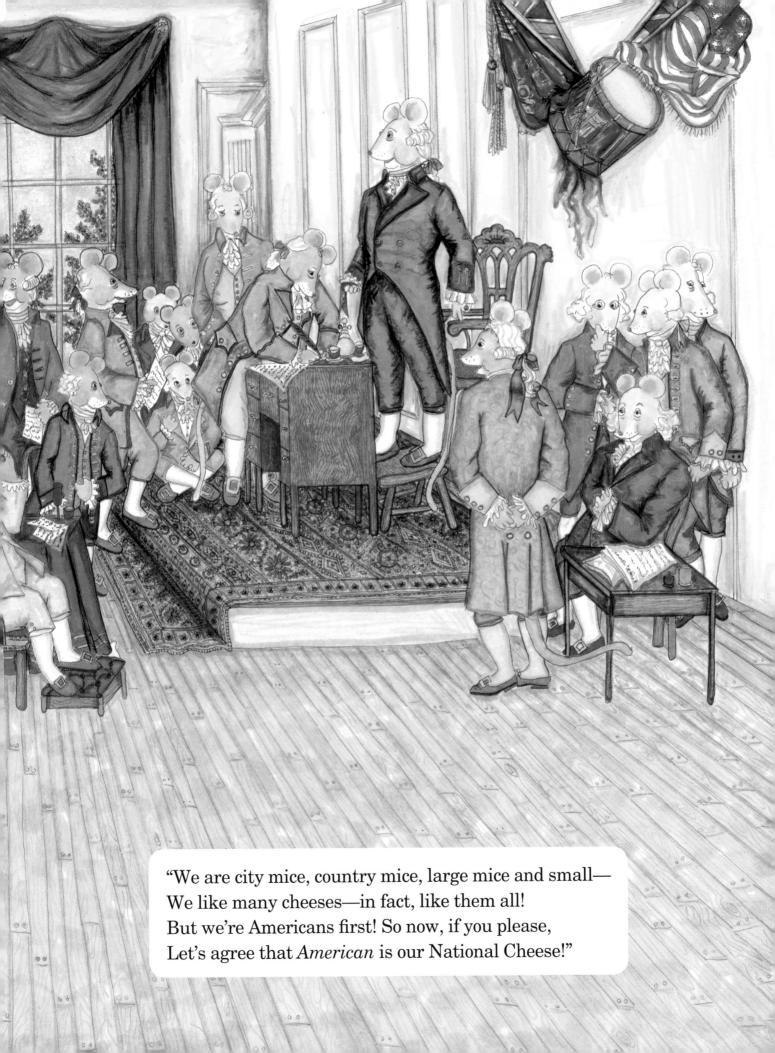

"We are city mice, country mice, large mice and small—
We like many cheeses—in fact, like them all!
But we're Americans first! So now, if you please,
Let's agree that *American* is our National Cheese!"

# The Oval Office

"Bravo!" they all shouted. "Hooray!" they yelled twice.
"What a good compromise, what terrific advice!"
In the House and the Senate, it passed right away,
And the president signed it the very next day!

And back in Moussouri, where everything started,
Miss Tuftmouse's class was very glad-hearted.
"Look, children, look," she said, "isn't it grand?
We live in a wonderful, wonderful land!"

# The Tail End
## Resources for Parents and Teachers

In 1792, the new government of the United States held a contest for the design of a Capitol for the young nation. William Thornton, a doctor and amateur architect, submitted the winning design, and in September 1793, President Washington laid the cornerstone of the building. The north wing was the first part finished, in 1800. In 1807, the south wing was completed. The two wings were separated by a vacant yard that was the site for the domed center.

By 1811, most of the work on the two wings was done. But war with England was imminent, so the Americans ceased further construction. In 1814, during the War of 1812, the British captured Washington, D.C., and set fire to the Capitol and other buildings. The structures were saved from total destruction only by a sudden rainstorm.

The reconstructed wings of the Capitol were reopened in 1819. The center opened in 1826, joining the two wings. The original dome was low, built of copper and wood. But by 1850, with the nation growing so quickly, the government had approved plans to design and construct two new, larger wings to accommodate the expanding Congress. The architects quickly realized that the longer building would make the low dome look out of proportion, so Congress appropriated additional money for a new, taller dome. The House moved into the new south wing in 1857; the Senate moved into the new north wing in 1859. Work on a tall cast-iron dome continued during the Civil War, and it was finished and capped with the Statue of Freedom in late 1863. Despite the war, President Lincoln insisted that the construction go on—he felt the work would be a symbol to the people that the Union would go on as well.

Illustrator Cheryl Shaw Barnes spent many days on Capitol Hill researching the art and architecture of the buildings there for this book. She also consulted with historians and curators of the House, Senate, and Capitol. All of the illustrations are based on actual structures, rooms, furnishings, and artwork.

In this book, the United Mice of America have built their own miniature Capitol. Our Capitol building is a work of art, with many painted walls and frescoes; famous paintings, statues, and sculptures are everywhere. The building has a floor area of 16.5 acres, and has 540 rooms, 658 windows, and 850 doorways. Later in the story, the children's letter arrives in the House mail room. At the time of the authors' research, the mail room was located in the Longworth House Office Building on Capitol Hill. Now it is located in the nearby Ford House Office Building. The Longworth Building is still home to the beautiful Ways and Means Committee Room, where the congressmice reviewed the National Cheese bill.

Unlike members of the House, senators have their own desks in the Senate chamber. Many of the desks have a special history. For example, in some, senators have carved their names in the desk drawers; one desk in the back row is the "Candy Desk," stocked with a good supply of sweets for members.

This story has some fun with some titles: "Squeaker of the House" is a play on "Speaker of the House," who is the top leader in that chamber. "Mouse-jority Leader" is a play on "Majority Leader," who is the chief in the Senate.

In the story, when the bill is in trouble, the Squeaker and the Mouse-jority Leader meet in the magnificent President's Room, off the Senate floor. The room, known as the "Gem of the Capitol," was constructed in the 1850s and is decorated with frescoes and oil paintings (the portraits represent the members of George Washington's first cabinet). Until the 1930s, the room was often used by presidents for signing bills; the mahogany table they sat at still stands under the great crystal and bronze chandelier.

To settle the disagreement over the bill, the lawmakers gather in the mouse Capitol Rotunda. The real Rotunda is 96 feet in diameter; the canopy is 180 feet from the floor. In 1865, Italian-American artist Constantino Brumidi painted a 4,664-square-foot fresco on the canopy, *The Apotheosis of Washington*, which honors the life of the first president. Other famous works of art, including John Trumbull's *Declaration of Independence* (1819), hang from the Rotunda wall. In the story, the illustration of the mouse Founding Fathers is based on Howard Chandler Christy's *Scene at the Signing of the Constitution* (1940), which hangs in the east stairway of the House wing. The 20 x 30 foot canvas is the largest painting in the Capitol.

When the mouse Congress passes the National Cheese bill, members go to the White House for the signing ceremony in the Oval Office with the mouse president, Woodrow G. Washingtail. (He is the main character of the authors' first Washington, D.C., book, *Woodrow, the White House Mouse*.) Woodrow signs the bill at the Resolute Desk, a special desk used by many presidents over the years. It was built from the oak timbers of the British ship *Resolute*. The desk was given as a present to President Hayes by Queen Victoria in 1880, after the stranded ship was recovered in the Arctic by American whalers and returned to England.

*For more information on the Capitol, contact the office of your representative or senator, or the U.S. Capitol Historical Society in Washington, D.C., at http://www.uschs.org.*

# The Tail End
## Resources for Parents and Teachers

## How a Bill Becomes a Law

The idea for a bill can come from many places: a letter from a second grade class; a voter; a member of the House or Senate; or someone who works on a member's staff. But once the research is done, the bill can be introduced only by a member of Congress. The bill is first referred to a committee, a smaller group of members who specialize in the issue that is addressed in the proposed legislation—the House Ways and Means Committee, for example, specializes in taxes, health care, trade, welfare, and Social Security. But the committee usually refers the bill to an even smaller group, a subcommittee, for close review. The subcommittee or full committee will hold hearings on the bill, taking testimony or other input from experts, the administration, interest groups, and the public. Once the hearings are completed, the bill is "marked up" with changes and amendments. Then the bill is "reported out" of committee if it is approved by a majority of members. The bill is then put on the chamber calendar for debate and voting. Each bill must be approved by both chambers, often twice. The first time, each chamber usually votes on its own version of the bill. Then members from the House and Senate meet in a "conference committee" to negotiate the differences. Once they do, the bill is returned to each chamber for final approval and sent to the president, who can sign or veto it. If vetoed, a bill can still become a law with a two-thirds vote of each chamber of Congress.

*For more information on how bills become laws, contact the office of your representative or senator, or go online, to http://www.kids.gov.*

## Acknowledgments

We have many people to thank for their time and help in the production of this book, including: Richard Allan Baker, Richard C. Barnett, Charles M. Boesel, Tim Hanford, Barbara-Ann Hanrahan, Kelly D. Johnston, James "Ernie" LePire, Leigh Ann Metzger, Jim Miller, Diane K. Skvarla and her staff, Barbara A. Wolanin and her staff, and several other Capitol Hill staffers, who, in the best tradition of Washington, wish to remain anonymous.

## Appreciation

The authors wish to thank
all the members of the Senate and House
and their staffs, past and present,
as well as all the officers and employees of
the Congress of the United States,
past and present,
for their hard work and public service.

We would especially like to thank
Nancy Fleetwood Miller, who opened doors
and made introductions for us in the Congress.
She was Director of Congressional Affairs,
U.S. Department of Transportation, during
the Reagan administration and then served
as Special Assistant to President George H. W. Bush
at the White House. She and her husband Jim
have two daughters and live in Alexandria, Virginia.

—P. W. B. and C. S. B.